WONDERFUL WORLD

Pictured here are some of the amazing places, plants, and animals you'll read about in this book. Can you identify them?

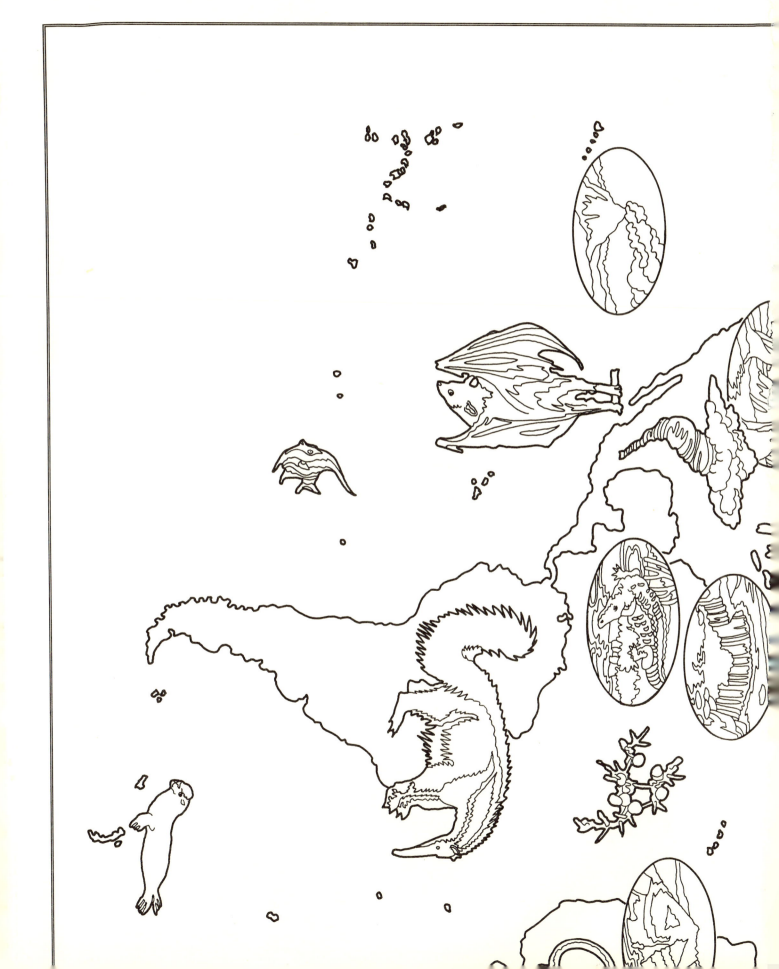

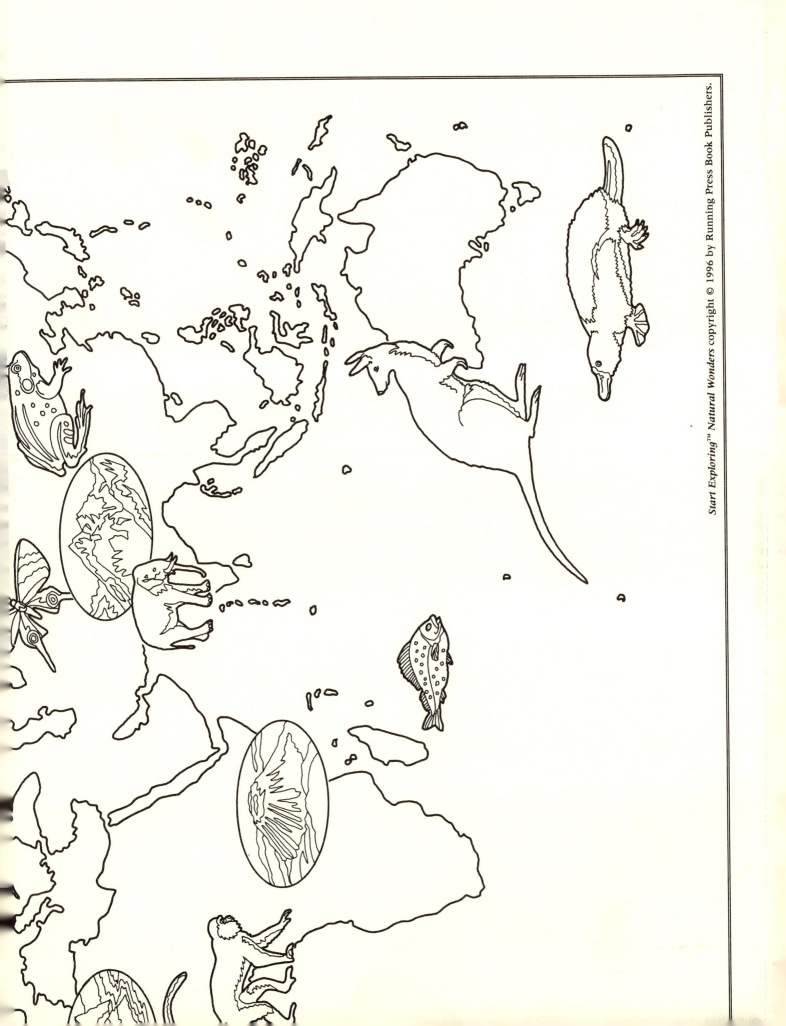

Start Exploring™

NATURAL WONDERS

A Fact-Filled Coloring Book

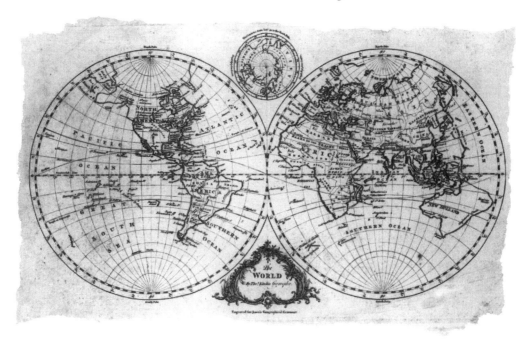

Elizabeth Corning (Bettina) Dudley, Ph.D.
Illustrated by Helen I. Driggs

RUNNING PRESS
PHILADELPHIA · LONDON

ISBN 1–56138–695–2

Cover design by Linda Chiu Barber
Interior design by Corinda J. Cook
Edited by Brian Perrin
Title page illustration by Thomas Kitchina, courtesy of the Library Company of Philadelphia.
Poster copyright © 1996 by Running Press.

This book may be ordered by mail from the publisher.
Please add $2.50 for postage and handling.
But try your bookstore first!
Running Press Book Publishers
125 South Twenty-second Street
Philadelphia, Pennsylvania 19103–4399

CONTENTS

Part 2: The Earth in Action

Part 3: Heavens Above!

Part 4: Wild, Wet, Wonderful Weather

Part 5: Wonderful Ways of Being

INTRODUCTION

Astronauts have circled the Earth and gazed back at it in awe from the surface of the moon. Scientists have sent space craft far out beyond the stars, but they have not yet discovered another place like our planet. As far as we know at this time, the Earth is the only place in the universe where life exists.

Billions of years ago, the Earth was only a hot ball of rock where no life could exist. Then, over time, the oceans developed. Early life began in the oceans. Many, many millions of years passed. More forms of life appeared, and the surface of the Earth as we know it began to take shape. Mountains and oceans came and went, continents moved together and drifted apart, glaciers advanced across the landscape and receded back again.

Today, this big, blue, beautiful ball is a truly remarkable place. Scientists have described more than 1.5 million kinds of plants and animals that share the Earth with us. Millions more remain to be discovered.

The Earth is endlessly full of surprises and delights—from the Dead Sea, far below sea level, to the heights of Mount Everest; from the depths of the ocean floor, miles below, to the waves washing the shore; and from the polar regions of the North and South to the rain forests around the equator.

The more we look, the more we realize that everything around us is a natural wonder just waiting to be seen.

NIAGARA FALLS
A Spectacular Border

Most borders between countries are just an imaginary line. But the border between the United States and Canada at Niagara Falls is one of the most spectacular sights in the world.

Honeymooners, school children and their families, visitors from faraway lands, and daredevils who want to ride over the falls in a barrel are among the thousands of sightseers who come to experience the power and grandeur of these mighty falls each year.

The falls at Niagara are made up of two distinct falls, separated by Goat Island. The American Falls, in New York state, are about a thousand feet wide. Large as they are, they're small compared to Ontario's Horseshoe Falls, which are more than one-half mile wide from side to side.

About twelve thousand years ago, the ice sheets that covered much of North America were melting. The icy waters flooded Lake Erie, which overflowed to form the Niagara River. Cutting through layers of limestone, sandstone, and shale, the river cascaded over a high cliff and formed Niagara Falls. Because the upper layer of this high cliff is made of very hard rock, an overhanging ledge formed, from which the falls drop straight down.

The river continues on through a seven-mile canyonlike gorge. You can stand on Rainbow Bridge, which spans this gorge, and have a great view of the falls. Visitors who dare to get closer can try the "Cave of the Winds," right behind the American Falls, or the steam ships that take you to the base of the falls. There you can experience up close the thundering power of this incredible wonder of nature!

THE GRAND CANYON

An Awesome Gorge

Two hundred and seventy-seven miles long, eighteen miles wide, one mile deep, and cutting through millions and millions of years of rock layers, the Grand Canyon is just that—GRAND.

There once was a time when the canyon didn't exist at all. Then, about six million years ago, the Colorado River began cutting through the rock layers that form the sides of the canyon today. The river cut deeper and deeper, eroding the rock further down toward the beginning of geological time.

As the river worked, so did the weather. The winds and rains gradually wore away the rock to make the canyon as wide as it is today.

It doesn't seem possible that a river could make such a deep and long canyon, even over millions of years. But the Colorado River is very, very fast and carries a lot of rock particles and mud called sediment. The river moves about five hundred thousand tons of sediment each day. This sediment helps the water scour and wear away the limestone and sandstone that form most of the rock layers.

There are great ways to see the Grand Canyon. Visitors can hike down to the river or ride down on horses or mules. Raft trips over the rough, churning white waters of the river provide a mixture of excitement and awe. Rafters have a great view of the splendid layers of red, brown, gray, pink, green, and violet rock rising up toward the clear blue sky.

While most people only visit, many animals live in the canyon itself or nearby. If you go there, look for bighorn sheep, elk, mountain lions, mule deer, pronghorn antelopes, and bobcats—they've all been seen in the area.

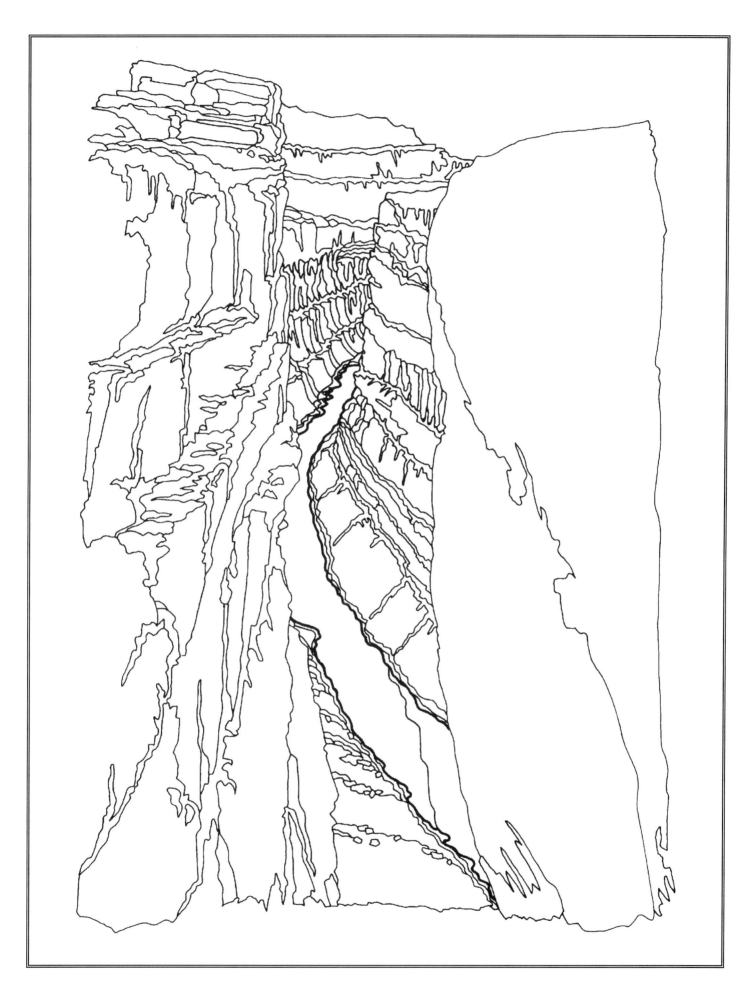

MOUNT EVEREST

The Highest Place on Earth

This is as high as you can get without leaving the ground. Rising 29,028 feet into the atmosphere, Mount Everest crowns the Himalayas—the mountains that divide Nepal from Tibet.

Everest stretches two thirds of the way up through the Earth's atmosphere. At that height, oxygen, which humans must breathe in order to survive, is greatly reduced.

Rocky and inhospitable, Everest's slopes are buffeted by gale-force winds and fierce snowstorms, and they are bitterly cold. Avalanches are commonplace. No plants or animals even attempt to eke out an existence here.

What a place! Why would anyone want to go there? "Because it is there," said Sir Edmund Hillary, the New Zealander who, along with Tenzing Norgay of Nepal, was the first to successfully climb to the top of Everest's summit ridge.

In 1852, scientists determined that this splendid peak was indeed the highest in the world. This news was enough to make mountaineers determined to climb its heights. It wasn't until after the First World War, nearly seventy years later, that the Dalai Lama—the religious leader of Tibet—granted permission for climbers to enter Tibet and approach the peak from the north. The first expedition failed to reach the top but learned much about the mountain for those who would follow. While some climbers came close, no one succeeded, and several men lost their lives in the attempt.

Finally, in 1949, after the Second World War, Nepal allowed expeditions to attempt a climb from the south. Four years later, a team approached along the Southeast Ridge, and two of its members—Hillary and Norgay—made it to the Earth's highest height. They stood high in the Himalayan skies, five and one-half miles up, and looked down on the rest of the world.

THE EVERGLADES
A River of Grass

Dawn comes quietly to the Everglades, that expanse of shining water and grasslike sedges that stretches a hundred miles from Lake Okeechobee to the tip of the Florida peninsula. The sawgrass is still in the morning calm. Before light only an occasional owl in the distance or a frog in a nearby slough disturbs the silence. Then, as the sun touches the palm trees growing on the hammocks, the landscape comes to life.

Deer move daintily past the cutting edges of the sawgrass, grazing on more tender shoots. Alligators stir sleepily. Now and then a bull alligator roars in his territory. A rare Florida panther moves from one hammock to the next. Birds fly from their nighttime roosts to their feeding grounds. Herons, egrets, and wood storks shine white against the clear sky. Roseate spoonbills reflect the sun in a blaze of color. Everglade kites and ospreys soar high overhead, looking down for prey.

There is no other place like the Everglades. This river of grass—a shallow waterway, often only a few inches deep—flows slowly down the miles to empty into the Gulf of Mexico. Moving steadily over porous, rough limestone, it forms a unique habitat as it flows.

The Everglades shelter familiar plants and animals from North America. They're also home to more exotic, tropical animals from South America, who come here to find their northernmost refuge.

If the water were to disappear, so would the hundreds of species of plants and animals that live there, and the dawn would seem barren. Luckily, many people care deeply about the Everglades and know how important it is to protect this natural wonder that is also a national treasure.

OUT AND ABOUT IN THE EVERGLADES

Sedge: A grasslike plant growing in damp places. Its stems have a triangular shape in cross section.

Sawgrass: The main grasslike plant of the Everglades, with sharp, cutting, sawlike teeth on its edges.

Slough: An open swampy place.

Hammocks: Tree-covered, elevated patches of ground.

Heron: Largest of the wading birds in the Everglades. It feeds on fish, frogs, and crayfish.

Egret: A small wading bird.

Wood Stork: A large wading bird that nests in colonies in the Everglades.

Roseate Spoonbill: A bright pink wading bird, with a flat, spoon-shaped bill.

Everglade Kite: A bird of prey that eats only snails.

Osprey: A bird of prey that dives into the water to catch fish.

NATURAL BRIDGES

Built by Nature

The bridges we build are impressive. They take a long time to construct, and they require the knowledge and skill of many people. Nature is skilled at building bridges, too. While a natural bridge doesn't need any human help, it does take a long, long time to build.

Here's how it works: Over many thousands of years, water can work its way through soft rock, such as sandstone or limestone. Eventually, that rock is eroded away by the persistent action of the water. If there's a layer of harder rock—resistant to erosion—on top of the soft rock, the hard rock becomes a bridge as the soft rock erodes away. The bridge may be very wide, with nothing but open space beneath it for hundreds of feet.

Sometimes natural bridges form along the ocean as the action of the waves wears away the soft rock underneath a cliff. This creates a sea arch—a natural platform that reaches out over the ocean and plunges into the sea floor—a very impressive sight.

There are natural bridges east of the Mississippi River, such as the one on land near Lexington, Virginia, that Thomas Jefferson bought in 1775 for twenty shillings. But the most impressive natural bridges lie to the west, in Utah. There, two magnificent areas have been preserved to highlight natural bridges: Rainbow Bridge National Monument and Natural Bridges National Monument. At Rainbow Bridge National Monument, the bridge is 290 feet high and 275 feet wide. That's almost as high and wide as a football field is long!

Utah's Rainbow Bridge stands 290 feet tall.

DEATH VALLEY
Full of Surprises

Deserts are hot and dry with no flowers in sight, right? Sometimes. But if you had been in Death Valley in eastern California and western Nevada after the rains in 1973, 1988, or 1994, you would have thought you were in a botanical garden. There were flowers everywhere!

These were truly exceptional years, because that much rain almost never comes to Death Valley. When it does rain, flowers always appear.

Desert soils are filled with seeds. If you gathered up a square yard of soil from the harsh and arid desert environment, you would find thousands of seeds in it. The seeds are dormant—sort of like sleeping—during dry times, but when a good rain comes, they germinate, grow, flower, and set the next generation of seeds—all in a matter of weeks.

The flowers are spectacular and showy, more like what you would expect to see in a tropical landscape. But they don't last long. They develop new seeds quickly, while there's still moisture in the ground, then they die. It doesn't rain very often, or very predictably, in Death Valley, so the plants that grow there have to respond quickly when it does.

Trees and shrubs that flourish in Death Valley either have widely spreading roots that can get water from a large area or "tap roots" that go way, way down into the ground. You and I wouldn't do so well in the harsh and unpredictable environment of Death Valley, but desert plants have developed strategies that let them thrive.

DESERTS
Hidden Wonders

Have you ever been eating a dessert when you suddenly bit into something wonderful that you didn't know was there, such as a cherry or a piece of pecan? Deserts in the southwestern United States are full of such dessertlike surprises.

Stretching off into the horizon, shimmering in the sun, deserts are hot and dry places where cactuses, tumbleweed, rattlesnakes, and spiders live. Even these creatures, who are accustomed to the environment, seem hot and dry. Nothing soft and lush can last in the desert, or so it would seem.

Deep canyons with rapid rivers flowing through them often cut through deserts. Running into these canyons are smaller side canyons with streams that empty into the rivers. Every so often you can find a place where one of these streams becomes a waterfall, cascading over rocks into a pool below. These pools hold spectacular surprises.

Shaded by the canyon walls from the glaring heat of the sun, the pools and the rocks around them are havens for plants, birds, and animals you would never expect to find in the middle of the desert. Maidenhair ferns, soft and delicate, thrive in the gentle spray of the waterfall. Deep green mosses coat the rocks. Columbines, with their nodding red and white flowers standing out like beacons against the mossy backdrop, crowd every available ledge. Hummingbirds hover by the flowers. Frogs, fat and lazy, plop into the cold water of the pool where small fish swim. Northern waterthrushes look for insects at the pool's edge. Warblers sing at high noon in the shade of the canyon walls.

HYDROTHERMAL VENTS
Life in the Abyss

ar below the surface of the ocean, deep in the darkest depths where no sunlight ever shines, are hydrothermal vents that are home to a number of amazing animals. Hydrothermal vents are found in trenches in the ocean floor. They're cracks and rifts that open in the Earth's crust as it moves and spreads. When such a vent opens in the sea floor, water that has been heated to extremely high temperatures under the surface of the Earth flows out.

The hot water is rich in minerals and hydrogen sulfide. When it comes into contact with the nearly freezing ocean water, it cools from more than six hundred degrees Fahrenheit to a more livable, comfortable temperature.

When researchers in underwater vessels first saw a hydrothermal vent community, they were stunned. They saw hundreds of huge, blood-red worms living in white tubes up to twelve feet long. These worms were densely packed, living along with mussels, clams, and crabs, in an area where scientists previously thought nothing could live.

How do these animals survive in a world without sunlight? How do they get anything to eat? Scientists have learned that the bacteria living in hydrothermal vents are able to make their own food from the hydrogen sulfide in the water. They do this through a process called *chemosynthesis*. The clams and mussels then feed on the abundant bacteria.

The tube worms, which have no mouths or digestive system of any sort, are another story. At first no one could figure out how they eat. Now we know that their blood-filled red tentacles can absorb molecules of food and oxygen directly from the water. The worms' blood then carries the nourishment throughout their bodies.

The unique and amazing creatures living in hydrothermal vents are able to live completely self-sufficiently. Some create their own food, and all survive in a deep abyss, far away from the rest of the world.

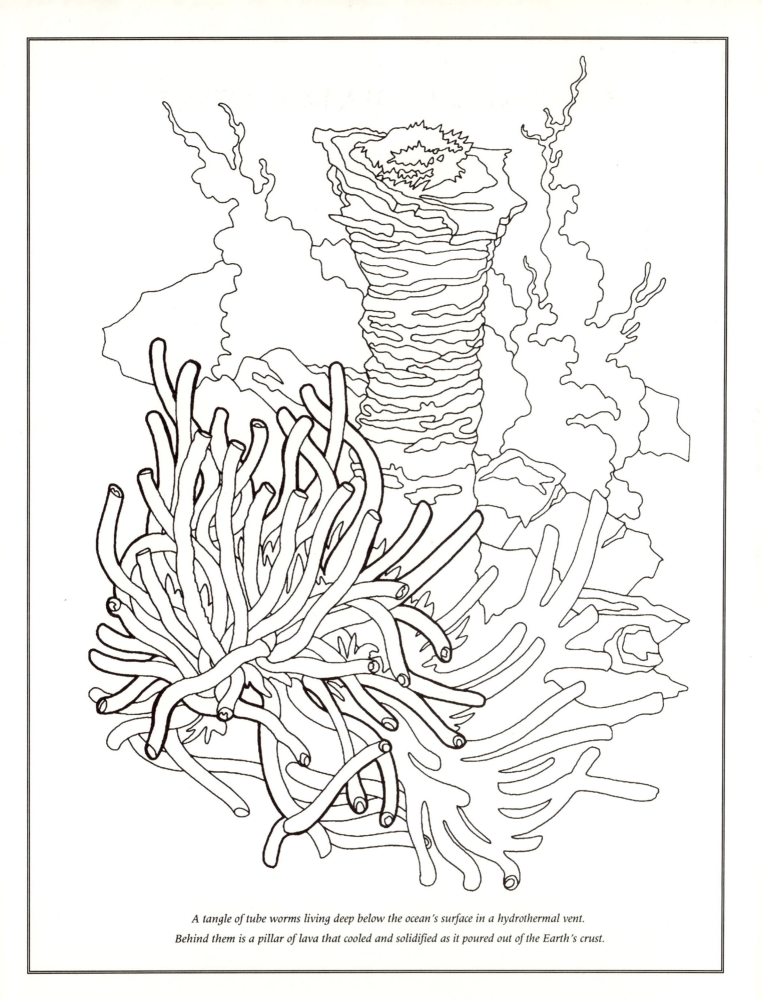

A tangle of tube worms living deep below the ocean's surface in a hydrothermal vent.
Behind them is a pillar of lava that cooled and solidified as it poured out of the Earth's crust.

PRAIRIES
Seas of Grass

When Europeans first arrived in America and began to move west, they came upon a land covered with tall, tall grasses. As the wind blew across the endless expanses, the movement of the grass resembled the waves of an immense ocean.

Prairies flourished all across the West, from central Texas to southwestern Saskatchewan in Canada, over most of Oklahoma, Kansas, Nebraska, Iowa, Illinois, South Dakota, North Dakota, Alberta, and Manitoba.

Prairies had dark, fertile soil formed by the decay of generation after generation of grass roots. Periodic fires cleared away dead plant material and returned more nutrients to the soil. Dozens of kinds of grasses and hundreds of species of flowers flourished there. From April to November, thousands upon thousands of colorful blooms—yellow, orange, red, and purple—formed a dazzling mosaic against the green grass. Jack rabbits, deer, elk, antelope, prairie dogs, and bison thrived, feeding on the lush plants of the world's most fertile lands.

Where are the prairies today? Where can you go to see huge herds of bison grazing peacefully in the waving grass? Sadly, little is left of this once-flourishing ecosystem.

Because the prairie soil was so fertile, it was perfect for farming. As more and more settlers arrived in the West, they converted the prairies into farmland. Over time, cities and roads were built, displacing still more prairie lands. There once were more than 140 million acres of tall grass prairie. Today less than one-tenth of that remains.

For the past fifty years, people have been working to restore the prairies. While prairie land will never again be as rich and endless as it once was, there are still some places you can go today to see a sea of ten-foot tall grass blowing in the breeze as bison graze peacefully in the sun.

THE SARGASSO SEA
An Ocean Desert

In the Atlantic Ocean near the Bermuda Islands lies an incredible area of dark blue, translucent waters. The waters here are so clear that light can shine deep below the surface—down as far as 3,300 feet!

Drifting on the gentle waves of these waters is a plant called the "sargassum" or "gulf weed." Many tons of the plant float freely, drifting with the currents. There is so much sargassum weed here that the area is known as the "Sargasso Sea."

The Sargasso Sea, in some ways, is like an ocean version of the desert. It has very weak currents and gets little rain. This means that when water from the surface evaporates, very little new water comes to the sea to replace it.

When water evaporates it leaves behind its salt content. Because evaporated water in the Sargasso Sea is not replaced by new water flowing in, the water in the area has an unusually high salt content. The temperature of the water there is also considerably higher than that of the surrounding ocean.

The result of all this is that plankton cannot live in the Sargasso Sea. Plankton are microscopic plants and animals that are the beginning of the marine food chain. Small fish eat plankton to survive, then larger fish eat the small fish, and so on. Without plankton, there are few fish or other animals in the Sargasso Sea, because there's simply not enough to eat.

Just as some land creatures have learned to live in the desert, however, a few animals have learned to survive in the Sargasso Sea. For example, the sargassum fish, which looks just like a piece of seaweed, floats on the surface and waits for unsuspecting prey.

A sargassum fish camouflaged among the sea weed of its salty ocean home, the Sargasso Sea.

THE GREAT BARRIER REEF

The Largest Living Structure on Earth

Tiny creatures working hard for thousands of years have built a complex community along a 1,250-mile strip off the northeastern coast of Australia. This is the Great Barrier Reef, the largest biological structure in the world, built by bryozoans (small, mosslike animals), corals, and algae.

A biological structure is one that is made up of living or once-living material, or from the byproducts of a living organism, such as the skeletons of coral. The Great Barrier Reef is eighty thousand square miles in area—so big that it can be seen clearly from the moon! The amazing thing about this huge structure is that it was built by animals and plants so small that some of them can only be seen through a microscope.

Most corals and many kinds of algae build protective skeletons of calcium carbonate (limestone), which they draw from the warm Australian waters. When the builders die, their skeletons remain in place or drift down to the bottom of the ocean. Over time this material builds up into an enormous structure that continues to grow, slowly but surely.

The reef then protects the creatures that build it and becomes a haven for thousands of other organisms, as well. More than fifteen hundred kinds of fish live there, along with worms, lobsters, crayfish, shrimp, and crabs. These creatures provide a remarkable underwater show, making the Great Barrier Reef a very popular place for scuba divers.

Some of the reef islands have become nesting grounds for giant green turtles. One beach is visited by ten thousand of these enormous turtles each night, when they come to lay their eggs. Some of the turtles weigh as much as five hundred pounds!

THE BAY OF FUNDY

Enormous Tides and Moving Waterfalls

On October 5, 1869, a powerful storm moved up the eastern coast of North America, bringing gale-force winds to Canada's Bay of Fundy. The Saxby Gale, as the storm was called, also brought to the bay the highest tide the world has probably ever known. It was more than seventy feet high—taller than a lot of apartment buildings!

The reason this tide was so high has to do with the way the Bay of Fundy is shaped. Wide and open to the ocean at its mouth, the bay gets increasingly narrow as it moves inland. At its head—the area that is most inland, known as the "Minas Basin"—more than one-half mile of tidal flats is exposed at low tide. (Tidal flats are stretches of land that are exposed when the tide is out, but covered with water during high tide.)

During an ordinary high tide, the water that enters the mouth of the bay sweeps up through the channel of the bay into the narrow Minas Basin, rising more than fifty vertical feet. During storms such as the Saxby gale, the volume of water that enters the bay is much higher than normal—and so are the tides.

The way the water travels in the bay is also very unusual. Because the tide moving from the mouth of the bay has more water in it than can be held at the head, the shallow water is overtaken by the deeper water moving in from behind. This forms a "tidal bore," which looks like a huge, traveling waterfall, moving at speeds up to eight miles an hour. To people watching from the shore, it's an amazing sight to see an enormous waterfall racing up the bay to fill the Minas Basin!

At low tide, the water level in the Bay of Fundy drops so low that this boat almost rests on the floor of the bay.
But when the tide is in, the boat floats high enough to reach the dock.

THE AMAZON RIVER

A River That Sets Many Records

High in the Andes Mountains in Peru, the Amazon River begins as a series of small streams and rivers. As they flow down through the lands once farmed by the ancient Incas and across the South American continent, these rivers are joined by others to become the largest river in the world.

Almost twenty-five percent of all the water that runs off the Earth's surface is carried by the Amazon River. It drains 2,700,000 square miles of land, including half of Brazil and parts of eight other South American countries. Eleven hundred smaller rivers, seventeen of them more than 1,000 miles long, drain into the Amazon before it reaches the end of its four-thousand-mile journey at the Atlantic Ocean on Brazil's northeast coast. This is a mighty river indeed!

During the course of the Amazon's journey, it travels through the world's largest tropical rain forest. It floods large areas of this forest every year, providing fertile soils in which a multitude of trees flourish.

Muddy and rich, the waters of the Amazon are home to three thousand known species of fish, including the pirarucu—the world's largest freshwater fish— electric eels, and giant catfish that weigh several hundred pounds. South American crocodiles called "caimans," manatees, and pink dolphins also swim in its waters. Giant anacondas (the world's largest snakes, big enough to swallow prey weighing 150 pounds), monkeys, anteaters, and exotic tropical birds all live in the trees on the Amazon's shores.

As you can see, the Amazon is a wonder in its own right. It's also a magnificent place to see many of nature's most amazing plants and animals.

RAIN FORESTS
Wonderlands of Exotic Life

Tropical rain forests are home to an amazing number of different plants and animals. While rain forests cover only about seven percent of the land on Earth, scientists think that half of the plants and animals found on land live in tropical rain forests. This is one reason that so many people fight to save the world's rain forests from disappearing.

In a ten-minute walk through a northern hardwood forest, you might see ten or fifteen different species of trees, a climbing vine or two and some shrubs, half a dozen mammals, twenty birds, and a few butterflies, bugs, and bees.

A similar walk through a rain forest would be a very different adventure. To begin with, the dense tangle of shrubs, vines, and flowering plants makes it almost impossible to *walk* through a rain forest. But if you could, you might walk past a hundred different kinds of trees in ten minutes. These would be covered with dozens of different mosses, lichens, ferns, orchids, and other epiphytes (plants that grow on other plants).

You might also see thousands of different animals. Barro Colorado is a small island in the Panama Canal, only one-tenth the size of Washington, D.C. In its rain forest, scientists have found 1,400 different kinds of plants, 444 species of birds, 500 different kinds of butterflies, more than 100 kinds of frogs, lizards, and snakes, forty-five species of bats, and forty-five other mammals. One scientist studied the insects living on just one species of tree and found 1,100 different kinds!

So, while a northern forest might have as many as 100 different kinds of organisms, a rain forest can have more than 3,600. That's 360 times as many!

THE NORTH POLE
One Long Day and One Long Night

If you lived in the Arctic—the region around the North Pole—your year would be divided into one day and one night. From March 21 to September 23—the arctic summer—the sun never sets completely. For the rest of the year, it never rises!

The word "arctic" calls up an instant image of ice. But should it? In contrast to the Antarctic, or South Pole, more than sixty percent of the Arctic is ice-free.

The Arctic Ocean, bordered on the south by Greenland and the northern parts of Europe, Asia, and North America, is roughly centered on the North Pole. It's covered by a nine-foot layer of pack ice almost all year long.

Some parts of arctic land masses have glaciers surrounded by permafrost (permanently frozen ground). Other places have summer temperatures higher than sixty degrees Fahrenheit. With these temperatures, many people are happy to live in the Arctic, and some cities have been there for a very long time.

Plants and animals are happy there, too. In the southern regions, or "low Arctic," there are small shrubs, mosses, grasses, and lichens. In summertime the land is covered by fields of flowers. In the northern regions, or "high Arctic," the tundra—a frozen, treeless place—has low-growing flowering plants and mosses. The "polar desert"—the land nearest the North Pole—is dotted with ground-hugging cushion plants.

All these plants provide food for grazers such as musk-oxen, caribou, and reindeer. Arctic wolves and foxes, polar bears, martens, and snowy owls feed on small animals, such as lemmings. Many species of birds nest in the arctic plants and raise their young quickly during the short arctic summer. The Arctic is actually a pretty busy place!

THE SOUTH POLE
An Antarctic Land of Ice and Snow

Antarctica—the continent around the South Pole—is truly a frozen land. Seventy percent of all the world's fresh water is frozen solid here. In some places, the ice cover is nearly three miles thick!

Antarctica is one and a half times larger than the United States. Ninety-eight percent of the continent is permanently covered with ice and snow. It is surrounded by seas that are covered for miles and miles by ice.

Fossils of trees, dinosaurs, and small mammals tell us that once, long ago, it was warmer in Antarctica. Today only two species of flowering plants live here, and the largest land animal is a wingless fly that is less than half an inch long. Larger animals can be found along the coastline.

The coldest temperature the world has ever known was recorded here, on July 21, 1983, at Vostok, high on the Antarctic Plateau. That day, the temperature dropped to -128.6 degrees Fahrenheit.

At the South Pole, the mean temperature is -58 degrees Fahrenheit. When it's that cold, you can throw boiling water up into the air, and watch it explode into ice crystals before it hits the ground!

Things are a bit warmer along the coast of the continent, where temperatures are around freezing (32 degrees Fahrenheit) during the summertime. There, penguins nest along the shore or on the sea ice (which is sometimes warmer than the land!). Seals, killer whales, and gigantic blue whales all can be seen swimming in coastal waters. These creatures don't seem to mind the cold, but it's certainly not the best place for humans to go to the beach!

CAVES
Mysteries of the Subterranean World

Books and movies are full of stories about fantastic caves so big that people get lost in them and have incredible adventures. There really are caves like that, formed in limestone and other kinds of soft rock. They're fascinating places.

Limestone is dissolved easily by ground water trickling down from the surface of the land. The water carries carbon dioxide from the air and the surface soil. The carbon dioxide forms a mild acid that helps dissolve the rock. Over many, many years, the rock is worn away, and caves form, often with underground streams in them.

Caves can be very small—just big enough to stand up in—or very large. The Monmouth-Flint Ridge cave system in Kentucky extends more than 190 miles!

Caves are full of stunning natural structures, known as "speleotherms," that form from mineral deposits. Stalactites are iciclelike deposits that hang from the ceiling; stalagmites are pillars that rise up from the floor. Sometimes stalactites and stalagmites reach out and join together to form great, cathedral-like columns.

The mysterious, dark depths of caves also hide many living wonders. Birds, salamanders, insects, spiders, bats, and some mammals live there. Sometimes bears spend the winter in caves.

Way at the back of some caves, where it's totally dark and the temperature and humidity always stay the same, you can find animals called "troglobites." Troglobites *never* see the light of day. They're usually blind, but they have a very well-developed sense of touch and smell. Their skins or shells are thin and pale. Cavefish—one kind of troglobite—have no eyes and no skin color, but they have touch organs all over their bodies that help them feel the things around them.

THE GREAT SALT LAKE
Thick Water

If you've ever gone swimming in the ocean, you've probably noticed that it's much easier to float there than in a freshwater lake. That's because salt water is denser—thicker—than fresh water. The thicker the water, the more weight it can support.

If you ever go swimming in Utah's Great Salt Lake, you'll find it really easy to float there. The Great Salt Lake has so much salt in its waters that it is even denser than the ocean.

Oceans are about two and one-half percent salt and one percent other minerals. These minerals come from the land. They are washed into rivers when it rains, and the rivers carry them into the oceans.

The Great Salt Lake is much saltier than any ocean. Streams and rivers drain into it, but there is no stream or river that carries water and minerals out again. Eighteen million tons of minerals pour into the Great Salt Lake every year, but they never wash out. The water evaporates, but the minerals remain. As a result, the salt content can be as high as twenty-seven percent—ten times higher than ocean water!

This is the largest inland saltwater lake in the western hemisphere, but its size changes with the weather. It can expand to an area of 2,400 square miles or shrink to only 950 square miles, depending on how much rain falls in surrounding areas. If you wanted to build a cottage on the shore of the Great Salt Lake, you'd have a hard time figuring out where to put it.

Huge crystals of salt form on these branches floating in Utah's Great Salt Lake.

POTHOLES, PONDS, AND ROADSIDE DITCHES
Disappearing Waters, Disappearing Homes

If you look in a puddle, a small pond, or a roadside ditch filled with water, you might see clumps of frog eggs or long strings of toad eggs. These are risky waters: the hundreds of tadpoles that hatch from the eggs can't survive if they dry up.

As the water begins to dry, you can watch the tadpoles crowd closer and closer. Sometimes the water lasts long enough for all of the tadpoles to turn into frogs or toads and hop away. Other times the water evaporates before the tadpoles can grow up, and most of them die.

Fairy shrimp—small, delicate crustaceans that often live in water-filled potholes—lay two kinds of eggs as a way of dealing with dry spells. One kind of egg hatches as soon as even the smallest amount of rain falls in the pothole. The other kind won't hatch unless it gets wet more than once.

When a rain comes, the first eggs hatch. If all of the water in the pothole evaporates before the shrimp can grow up and lay their own eggs, there's still another chance. If more rain comes, the second eggs hatch. This time, with luck, there's enough rain to last until the shrimp are fully grown.

The wonderful thing is that some of the creatures living in disappearing waters do survive to lay their own eggs the next spring.

EARTHQUAKES

Shake, Rattle, and Roll!

As people in San Francisco or Los Angeles know all too well, when the dishes start rattling an earthquake is happening.

There are as many as a million earthquakes each year, but you won't hear about most of them. This is because most earthquakes occur beneath the sea, where we don't notice them. On land, they can be truly devastating, and not just to dishes, houses, and freeways. A 1976 earthquake in China killed 250,000 people, and that was only a medium-size quake.

Have you ever wondered about what causes an earthquake? It's pretty amazing: the crust of the Earth is moving. The crust is made up of huge pieces called "tectonic plates." These plates are always moving slowly—so slowly we don't even notice.

In weak areas of the Earth's crust, or "faults," the plates press together and exert strong pressure on the rocks at the plates' edges. If the force gets to be too much, the rocks break and move. The resulting energy travels in waves, vibrating and shaking whatever it travels through. When this happens, you've got an earthquake.

The size and force of an earthquake are often measured on a scale called the "Richter scale." Each point on the scale represents a huge increase in the size of the quake. An earthquake that registers 2.5 is very small. Such tiny tremors happen frequently. A quake that measures 6 is very destructive, and a 7 is a major quake.

The place where a quake begins, deep within the Earth, is called the "focus." The point on the Earth's surface directly above the focus is called the "epicenter." Major earthquakes have been known to shake cities hundreds of miles away from the epicenter!

TIDAL WAVES
Great Walls of Water

Huge tidal waves, known technically as "tsunamis," are another disaster that can happen after an earthquake. Usually, tidal waves are caused by earthquakes that take place under the ocean, but some quakes on land near a coast can also set off these enormous waves.

Like the ripples that form after a rock is thrown into a pond, a tsunami travels outward from its starting point. It can travel for thousands of miles. An earthquake on the Alaskan coastline can cause a tidal wave in Hawaii, for example.

If you were on a boat on the open ocean, you might not even notice a tsunami passing by. While a tsunami is traveling through deep water, its waves are very long—anywhere from sixty to 120 miles—but only one to two feet high.

But don't ever be near the beach when a tsunami is coming! As it approaches the shore, the wave is slowed by the sea floor and becomes higher and higher. The water at the shore might first recede, going much further out than the lowest of low tides. Then the tidal wave rushes in with great speed, destroying everything in its path.

Scientists can roughly predict when a tsunami will reach the shore. For every minute it takes for the tremors from the tsunami-causing earthquake to reach the shore, it will take an hour for the actual wave to arrive. So, if the earthquake tremors arrive ten minutes after the quake began, you can predict that the tidal wave will arrive in about ten hours. Being able to predict how long it will take for the wave to arrive allows time to get people to safety. In earlier times, people didn't know a tidal wave was coming until it was too late.

VOLCANOES

Mountains That Spit Fire and Ash

A quiet volcano looks peaceful, but appearances are deceiving. Mount Vesuvius, a famous volcano in Italy, had been quiet for so many centuries that it was overgrown with plants all the way to the top. It seemed like an ordinary mountain. Then, in 63 A.D., some minor earthquakes occurred around the mountain. No one living nearby was particularly concerned. They didn't know the quakes had re-awakened the sleeping, or dormant, volcano.

Sixteen years later, in 79 A.D., the residents of the nearby village of Pompeii were overcome by poisonous fumes. Hot ashes completely covered the city, filling the streets up to the second floor of the houses. A sudden rainstorm turned the dust in the air to mud, and the villagers were buried by a rain of mud. Their bodies left impressions in the mud. In this century, scientists have made plaster casts from these impressions. The casts show us what the bodies of people who died two thousand years ago looked like.

A major volcanic eruption, such as the one that destroyed Pompeii, is truly terrifying. Fiercely hot, glowing clouds spread far and wide, carrying dust, ash, rock fragments, and poisonous gases. Rivers of lava, made of molten rock pushed up from far below the Earth's surface, travel as fast as seventy miles an hour. The lava flows down the slopes of the volcano, covering and destroying everything in its path. Volcanic ash is carried thousands of miles by the wind, darkening the sky and blocking out the sun. Mudflows form on the already devastated volcanic slopes. The mud flows for miles, coating roads, buildings, and countryside.

FAMOUS VOLCANOES TODAY

Volcano	*Location*	*Level of Activity*
Mt. Vesuvius	Naples, Italy	Still active; many major eruptions.
Mt. Fujiyama	Honshu, Japan	Dormant; last erupted 1707.
Mt. Kilimanjaro	Tanzania, Africa	Dormant.
Mt. St. Helens	Washington, United States	Active; last erupted 1980.
Mt. Rainier	Washington, United States	Dormant.
Mt. Erebus	Antarctica	Active; constantly puts off a plume of steam.
Krakatoa	Indonesia	Dormant; last erupted in 1883, sending ash around the world.

Indonesia's Mount Krakatoa.

51

GLACIERS
Ice on the Move

We don't usually think of ice as being something that moves or flows, especially not when we're ice skating on a frozen pond in the winter. But glaciers are just that—moving, flowing ice.

Glaciers are large masses of ice that are on the move all year long. In the Arctic and the Antarctic, glaciers are great sheets of ice. In high mountain valleys, they're narrower rivers of ice. There are even glaciers near the equator, on mountain peaks and in mountain valleys fifteen thousand feet high—almost three miles up.

A typical glacier can move as many as three feet each day. Some are much faster. For example, there are some in Greenland that move about 150 feet a day. And some glaciers have been known to move as much as fifteen feet in an hour for several weeks—not a good idea to get in their way!

In these places, more snow falls than can melt away in the summer months. Over the years, it builds up in layers, getting heavier and heavier and putting more and more pressure on the older layers of snow underneath. Eventually, the snow is compacted into crystals of glacial ice. When it becomes thick enough, this ice will move, pushed by the pressure of its own weight.

Icebergs come from glaciers. They're large pieces of ice that break away from glaciers at the sea's edge. This process is called "calving." In the Arctic alone, sixteen thousand icebergs are calved each year!

HOW TO MEASURE THE SPEED OF A GLACIER

The speed of a glacier can be measured by putting stakes in it.

Suppose you put a row of stakes in a straight line across a valley glacier, with the two end stakes on the valley walls. After a while you'd see something interesting: the stakes in the middle would have moved faster than the stakes on the sides. This is because the walls of the valley held the sides of the glacier back.

As a result, the line of stakes becomes U-shaped. You can measure how far the stakes in the middle of the line (now the curve of the U) have moved in comparison to the stakes at each end of the line. This will tell you about how far the glacier has moved since you put the stakes in it.

QUICKSANDS
Dangerous Ground

Have you ever been walking along the beach on the firm sand when it suddenly went soft beneath your feet? You might have sunk down several inches before your feet came into contact with solid ground once again.

What you experienced was a thin layer of quicksand. Quicksands can form in any sand where there's a lot of water between the sand grains. Sometimes the mixture of sand, mud, and vegetation in freshwater bogs can behave like quicksand, too. But usually, quicksands are found in places with a lot of very fine sand—in stream beds, in sand flats exposed at low tide on the seashore, and in the hollows at the mouths of big rivers.

When conditions are right, the water flows through the sand and forces the separate sand grains apart. As a result, the sand behaves like a liquid but looks like a solid. It can no longer support a heavy weight.

The thin layers of quicksand that sometimes occur on beaches aren't usually anything more than a little scary. A thick layer of quicksand can be dangerous, though—but only if you don't know what to do.

Because quicksands act like a liquid, you can actually float on them. If you ever fall into quicksand, spread out on your back and stretch your arms out. This distributes your weight so that you put less weight on any one spot. Once you've begun floating successfully, you can roll onto the safety of the firmer ground nearby.

GEYSERS
Great Steam Explosions

From the lava fields of Iceland to the green fields of New Zealand, geysers are acting up. All you have to do to see one is stand around and wait—but don't stand too close! Sooner or later, these hot springs will throw a great column of boiling water and steam up into the air.

Most geysers erupt without any particular schedule. Old Faithful is a different story, however. One of the most impressive of about two hundred geysers in Wyoming's Yellowstone National Park, Old Faithful has a very regular schedule. For the last eighty years, the geyser has erupted every seventy-three minutes on the button. You could set your watch by Old Faithful!

Geysers get their energy from deep within the Earth. The heart of a geyser is a channel that goes down far below the surface. Cold water pours into the channel from above. At the bottom of the channel, other water is heated by the extreme heat of the surrounding earth.

The pressure from the long column of water keeps the water at the bottom from boiling at first, but some of it does turn to steam. This steam pushes some water back up the column, allowing more of the water at the bottom to boil into steam. Finally, all the water at the bottom turns to steam and forces everything in the channel above it out of the mouth of the geyser in a great explosion. Then the process starts all over again.

If you're ever waiting for a geyser to erupt, you can pass the time by looking at the interesting formations around its mouth. As the hot water passes by rocks on its way to the surface, it dissolves chemicals and deposits them around the geyser's mouth. These deposits can make fascinating formations.

THE NORTHERN LIGHTS

Nature's Own Fireworks

If you like firework displays, you'd love the aurora borealis, or northern lights. For thousands of miles across Canada and the northern parts of the United States, when conditions are right, flickering arcs and folds of light cascade against the nighttime skies.

Rays of color, usually red, purple, or green, move up and down and across in an ever-changing show. The greenish rays can even be edged with a rippling red border, like a curtain on a celestial stage. As the show ends, the rays seem to dissolve into wide areas of white light. The experience is more spectacular than any Fourth of July fireworks.

The northern lights that we see here on Earth are actually caused by something that happens on the surface of the sun. Sudden explosions of energy, called "solar flares," release electrons and protons into a constant flow known as the solar wind. As these electrons and protons approach Earth, they strike oxygen and nitrogen atoms in the upper atmosphere. This causes radiation to be released in different wave lengths of bright and strong colors, producing the spectacular natural fireworks.

The aurora borealis is visible year in and year out, but it puts on its best show during the most intense phase of the eleven-year sunspot cycle. This is when sunspots—dark patches on the surface of the sun—become much more common than in other years. Solar flares are associated with sunspots, so they also become more common.

Watch for the aurora borealis far away from the lights of the city. The best place to see them is in the mountains, where there is only the light of the stars and the moon at night.

SOLAR ECLIPSES
Swallowing the Sun

The sky is darkening and the birds are beginning to sing their evening songs, but it's only the middle of the day. What's going on? Long ago in China, people thought a sky dragon was trying to swallow the sun. Today we know it's really a solar eclipse—one of the best natural shows around.

Solar eclipses take place at least twice a year somewhere in the world, but we're not often lucky enough to see them—you have to be in the right place at the right time. A solar eclipse lasts only a few minutes, but some people travel long distances to see them. As they watch, they see a dark outline of the moon appear on the sun's western side and move slowly across its face, blocking it from view.

When the moon has completely covered the sun, it appears to be surrounded by a bright halo. This halo is called the "corona" of the sun—its outer atmosphere. The sky is still blue, but dark, and it seems like night is about to come. Then, slowly, the moon moves off to the east. The whole eclipse lasts fewer than eight spectacular minutes.

If you happen to be in the right place to see an eclipse, remember not to look directly at it—not even through smoked glass or dark sunglasses. The rays of the sun, though shielded by the moon, can still do severe damage to your eyes. Use a pin-hole projector, such as the one shown here, to view the eclipse.

Pin-Hole Projector
Poke a tiny hole in a piece of paper and hold it up to the sun. Aim the hole at a wall or some other flat, clean surface, and watch as it projects a shadow of the eclipse in progress!

RAINBOWS

Bands of Colored Light

A heavy summer rain pours down. When it passes by, the sun comes out. Suddenly, a rainbow appears, stretching from horizon to horizon. An Irish legend says that there's a pot of gold at the end of every rainbow. A Native American legend says the flowers of the fields go into rainbows when they die. Rainbows are so beautiful, it seems as though both of these stories could be true.

Have you ever looked at light through a prism? Or maybe you have a "sun catcher," a crystal that breaks up sunlight into colors? The light that passes through these objects is "diffracted"—bent and broken down into the colors that make it up. When the light traveling from the sun hits the moisture in the air after a rain, the same thing happens. It gets diffracted into all the colors it's made of: violet, indigo blue, green, yellow, orange, and red. These colors make up the rainbow we see in the sky.

The color that any one raindrop reflects back to us depends on the angle between the sun and that drop. Many drops at different angles to the sun send different colors. Together, they make up all the bands of the rainbow.

Narrow bands of color in a rainbow come from larger raindrops. Wide bands come from smaller drops. Next time you see a rainbow, look at the width of the bands of light and try to guess what size raindrops it came from. Later, if you remember what this rainbow looked like, you can compare it to another rainbow and decide which one was caused by larger raindrops.

THE GREEN FLASH
A Rare Sight

One of the most interesting events in the sky happens so fast that you might miss it if you blink. It doesn't happen everywhere and it doesn't happen very often, so it's really an event to remember. It's known as the "green flash."

The time of day, the location, and atmospheric conditions all have to be just right. You can only see the green flash at sunrise or sunset. You have to be at the top of a high mountain, at the beach, or on a ship at sea, and you must have a wide, uninterrupted view of the distant horizon. In order for the green flash to occur, the sky must be completely clear, free of clouds and pollution.

If all of these conditions are just right, you might be lucky enough to see the green flash. It's a sudden, brief, and brilliant flash of green color that sometimes appears on the horizon just at the exact moment when the sun first begins to appear above the horizon in the morning, or just as the last glint of light disappears beneath the horizon in the evening. You have to be watching very closely, and you have to protect your eyes by not looking directly at the sun, so it takes perfect timing.

That's all there is to it—a brilliant green light caused by the bending of the sun's rays by the lower atmosphere. It's gone almost as soon as it appears, and maybe that's why it's so special. It's like catching a glimpse of a rare and beautiful bird. The experience is exciting and satisfying, but if we could see it every day, it might become ordinary and not special at all.

MIRAGES
Deceptive Light

Sometimes, when you're walking or driving down a hot road, you see a pool of water lying ahead of you on the pavement. But when you get closer, the puddle has disappeared. What you saw was an optical illusion known as a "mirage."

The ocean and the desert are also good places to see mirages. A real oasis is a sort of island of water and vegetation in the middle of a desert. The most common mirage of all is to see an oasis, complete with palm trees, suddenly appear in the desert. Similarly, sailors at sea have seen mirages of islands floating in the sky.

All mirages are caused in the same way—by the bending of light rays passing through air of different temperatures. The ground and the air above it heat up as the sun beats down. Light coming from the sky first comes through the cooler air high above the ground, then hits the hot air nearer the ground. The speed of the light increases in this hot air. This makes the light change its direction and bend upward as it reaches the ground.

When we see the light that has changed direction, it appears to us to have come from the ground. The light of a water mirage in the road is blue, since it's really light that came down from the sky. To us, it looks like a puddle of water, not a "puddle of sky." Since the hot air also causes the rays of light to ripple, the water even appears to have waves.

One very rare type of mirage, called a "fata morgana," makes whole mountain ranges seem to appear where there are none, or makes castles appear to float in the air!

METEORS
Shooting Stars

On a hot summer's night when the moon isn't full and the light of the stars fills the sky, you can lie on your back and scan the sky for "shooting stars." All of a sudden, a streak of light flashes across the sky. It lasts only a brief moment, but sometimes it leaves a trail that lingers for several minutes.

These streaks of light are called meteors. They look like stars falling out of the sky, but they're not. They are actually caused by meteoroids—small pieces of matter coming into the Earth's atmosphere from outer space.

Meteoroids float freely in outer space, where there is no atmosphere. But when a meteoroid enters our upper atmosphere, it gets hot from friction—rubbing against the molecules in the air—and begins to glow. As it gets closer to Earth, where the atmosphere is thicker, the increased friction makes it burn at a white heat. This is what creates the streak of light we see in the sky.

You might think meteoroids are very large, but in fact, most are no bigger than a grain of sand!

Many meteoroids coming into our atmosphere at the same time produce "meteor showers." On November 13, 1833, there was a spectacular display during what is known as the "Leonid shower." Hundreds of thousands of meteors streaked across the sky in a single night. People everywhere in North America saw the show. It was caused by meteoroids that came from a great ring of particles that is always revolving around the sun. We encounter the Leonid shower every year, but it has never been as impressive as on that night in 1833.

COMETS

Blazes of Light

Every once in a while we're lucky enough to see a comet, its tail a blaze of light across the sky.

On November 18, 1833, Halley's Comet—the most famous comet of all—appeared so brightly that people thought it meant the end of the world was near. Today we know a lot more about comets, and we know that Halley's Comet can be seen every seventy-seven years, when its orbit takes it closest to the sun. It was last seen in 1986, so we'll have to wait a long while to see it again!

All comets orbit around the sun. They have a head and a tail. At the core of the head is the "nucleus." The nucleus is made up of frozen gases and ice, mixed with fine, sootlike dust. Around the nucleus is the "coma"—a mixture of dust and gases turned into vapor by the sun's intense heat. The nucleus is usually about forty-five square miles. The coma is much bigger—up to 62,000 square miles. The tail, made up of gases and dust pushed from the comet's head, can be as many as 100 million miles long!

Because it's called a tail, you might think it always trails behind the head of the comet. When a comet is heading toward the sun, this is true: the tail is pushed behind by the sun's light. But when a comet moves away from the sun in the course of its orbit, the tail is pushed out in front.

Halley's Comet.

RAIN

A Water Wonder

Rain is essential because it's how we get our water. It's a big part of our lives, but we don't often stop to think just how important—or how incredible—it is.

If we lived in the desert in Chile that went without rain for fourteen years, we certainly would miss it. Or, if we were on Reunion Island in the Indian Ocean the day it rained seventy-four inches, we might have thought it was far too much of a good thing.

There is only as much water today as there ever was, or ever will be, on Earth. This water has to be used over and over again. In fact, when you get a glass of water from the kitchen sink, it's quite possible that a famous person—maybe George Washington or Marie Curie—drank some of that same water some time in the past. Many people have used the water in your glass.

When rain falls, much of it goes into the ground and then into streams, river, and lakes. From there, it is carried out to the oceans. The sun evaporates the water from the oceans—turns it to vapor—and draws it up into the atmosphere. Sooner or later, the water falls back to Earth as rain. This course of events is called the "hydrological cycle." Without this cycle, there could be no life on Earth, because nothing can live without water.

WATER WORLD

• Water covers about three-fourths of the Earth's surface.

• Only three percent of all water on Earth is fresh water.

• Three-fourths of that three percent is frozen in at the North and South poles or in glaciers.

• Rivers and lakes contain only one-fiftieth of one percent of Earth's water.

• Humans are made up of sixty-five percent water.

• Each person in the United States uses, on average, one hundred gallons of water each day.

THUNDERSTORMS

Huge Clouds, Loud Noises, and Lots of Electricity!

It's a gorgeous summer day. Off on the horizon are huge clouds. These giants, sometimes more than seven miles in height, are called "cumulonimbus clouds." They're also known as "thunderheads," because they're where thunderstorms start.

Inside these clouds, static electricity builds up. You've probably experienced static electricity at home. When you walk across the carpet in sneakers, you build up static electricity in your body. Then, when you touch another person or a metal object, a spark jumps from your finger and you feel a shock.

Lightning bolts are giant sparks of static electricity. A large negative charge builds in the lower portion of thunder clouds, and a positive charge builds in the upper part. When the difference between positive and negative becomes great, the charge jumps from one area to another, creating a lightning bolt.

Lightning bolts also may leap to other clouds or to the ground. They travel at the speed of light and discharge up to 100 million volts of electricity, heating the air around them to temperatures of up to 55,000 degrees Fahrenheit. This heat causes the air to expand rapidly in an explosive clap we hear as thunder.

Light and sound travel at different speeds. When you see lightning, count the seconds from the time you see it until you hear the thunder. Divide the number of seconds by five. This gives you a rough idea of how many miles away the storm is. When you hear the thunder and see the lightning at the same time, the storm is overhead.

Lightning can be dangerous, so it's a good idea to go inside during a thunderstorm. Don't stand under a tall, isolated tree. If lightning hits the tree, it could hit you, too. If you're in an open field and can't get inside, lie down in a low area.

TROPICAL STORMS

Violent Giants

Hurricane, cyclone, typhoon—three words with the same meaning: fiercely powerful tropical storms. Hurricanes occur in the north Atlantic and the eastern part of the North Pacific, cyclones take place in the Indian Ocean, and typhoons occur in the western Pacific. Some tropical storms never become hurricanes, cyclones, or typhoons.

Whatever they're called and wherever they are, these storms are an experience no one ever forgets. Sometimes the memories are of spectacular waves along a coast, of heavy rains followed by the clearest blue skies imaginable. But sometimes the memories are harsh—a severe tropical storm can be terribly destructive. Buildings can be flattened, roads washed out, forest trees broken like matchsticks, and lives lost.

Tropical storms start over an ocean in an area just north or south of the equator. They can grow to be as big as three hundred miles in diameter. The many clouds they carry produce heavy rains. Their fierce winds, with speeds greater than two hundred miles an hour, rotate counter-clockwise when they're north of the equator, clockwise when south of the equator. They stir up huge waves at sea and wreak havoc on land. In one day, an ordinary hurricane generates two hundred times as much energy as all the electrical power plants in the United States! Still, in the middle of all this awesome power, at the very center or "eye" of the storm, lies a cloud-free, clear place of calm.

HURRICANES THAT MADE HISTORY

Hurricanes are given human names, alternating between male and female and moving through the alphabet from A to Z each year. Here's a list of some hurricanes that are remembered for the massive destruction they caused:

Year	*Name*	*Principle Site of Damage*	*Year*	*Name*	*Principle Site of Damage*
1960	Donna	Florida to Maine	1974	Fifi	Honduras
1963	Flora	Haiti, Cuba, Dominican Republic	1979	David	Dominican Republic
1965	Betsy	Bahamas, Florida, Louisiana	1983	Alicia	Texas
1967	Beulah	Caribbean, Mexico, Texas	1988	Gilbert	West Indies, Mexico
1969	Camille	Louisiana to Virginia	1989	Hugo	West Indies, southeastern United States
1972	Agnes	Florida to New York	1992	Andrew	Florida

SNOW, SLEET, HAIL, AND GRAUPEL

Frozen, Falling Water

If the temperature of the Earth's atmosphere is cold enough, liquid water that might otherwise fall as rain can be changed into one of several solids: snow, sleet, hail, and even something we hardly ever hear about—graupel.

Graupel is best described as "snow pellets." These are created when snowflakes are hit by cloud droplets that freeze onto them. Graupel is softer than sleet, though not by much.

If you've ever been hit by sleet, you know it's not very soft. It's made of solid grains of ice less than one-fifth of an inch in diameter. It occurs when raindrops freeze or when partly melted snowflakes fall through freezing temperatures near the Earth's surface. Sleet will bounce on a hard surface and can sting if it hits you.

Hail can hurt, too. Hailstones are lumps of ice that started out as frozen raindrops—"hail embryos"—and grew when other water droplets froze on those embryos. Hailstorms often look like someone is throwing mothballs from the sky. The largest hailstone ever measured weighed one and two-thirds pounds and had a diameter of seventeen and one-half inches!

Snow—a much nicer thing to have fall on your head—is made from tiny crystals of ice. These crystals stick together and become snowflakes. Snowflakes always have six sides. They can be larger than one inch if lots of crystals have stuck together. It's said that no two snowflakes ever look the same.

TORNADOES

Twisting Terrors

The tornado that carried away Dorothy and her little dog Toto in *The Wizard of Oz* was just part of a story, but tornadoes are very real indeed. Their inward and upward whirling winds can easily carry away a car, to say nothing of a small dog.

Most tornadoes occur in the United States, in the midwestern states and those along the Gulf of Mexico. Warm and humid air from the gulf meets cool and dry air coming down from the north. At the place where they meet—called a "front"—huge cumulonimbus (thunderstorm) clouds form, and violent weather develops. When a rotating, twisting funnel cloud, looking a little like the trunk of an elephant, reaches down from those clouds, a tornado is happening. If you were nearby when this happened, you'd hear a tremendous noise—a hissing or whistling sound that would become an almost deafening roar when the tornado struck.

The most violent winds that occur anywhere in the world whirl around the center of these funnel clouds. The winds average speeds of three hundred miles an hour, but can go as high as five hundred! Luckily, a tornado only lives about an hour and only travels about twenty miles.

The damage in those twenty miles can be terrible. As a tornado passes over buildings, it sucks the air up from around them, causing air pressure to drop suddenly. The pressure inside the buildings stays the same as it was. This means the inside air pressure is suddenly greater than the outside air pressure. The inside air presses against the walls, and the buildings explode outward. Storm cellars or basements are the safest places to be when you know a tornado is coming—because they're underground, the walls are held together by the ground and they don't explode.

TYRANNOSAURUS REX

King of the Dinosaurs

Seventy million years ago, the world was a very different place. Hardly any of the animals we know today were alive then, but lots of dinosaurs roamed the land. Some were as small as little poodles, others were BIG. *Tyrannosaurus rex*, sixteen feet tall and ten thousand pounds, was the most striking of all.

Tyrannosaurus rex was a meat-eating dinosaur. Its heavily muscled head was more than three feet long, and its jaw was filled with huge, thick, dagger-sharp teeth. *Tyrannosaurus rex* could flex its jaw from side to side, instead of just open and closed. This helped it eat really big pieces of meat.

Its eyes faced forward, not out to the sides like those of its earlier relatives. This simple difference improved the dinosaur's depth perception. *Tyrannosaurus rex* was better than its ancestors at seeing its prey and figuring out how far away it was.

For front legs, *Tyrannosaurus rex* had only tiny limbs with traces of claws. Its hind legs, however, were tremendously strong and solid, with feet ideally built for running and dodging. This dinosaur was definitely a predator. It was ready to attack and ready to run.

Above all, it was ready to eat. Mostly it ate other dinosaurs, even though they were often heavily armored with protective plates, and had weapons like spikes, tail clubs, and horns. Because it was built for running, *Tyrannosaurus rex* could catch fast prey and avoid any counterattacks. Once it caught another dinosaur, its strong jaws and massive teeth made killing and eating very easy.

Tyrannosaurus rex was the perfect predator of its times. Do you wish it was still around today?

PTERODACTYLS

Flying Reptiles

About two hundred million years ago, one of the most amazing groups of animals ever known came into being. These were the hairy, flying reptiles called "pterodactyls."

About seventy million years ago, the most amazing pterodactyl of all lived in what is today the state of Texas. Scientists have found fossils of this gigantic creature in Big Bend National Park. The fossils show that it was forty feet across from wing tip to wing tip. This makes it absolutely the largest flying animal that has ever existed—it was as big as a twin-engine airplane. (Imagine looking out an airplane window and seeing it fly by!) Its head was eight feet long with sharp fangs and large jaw muscles. It had hardly any tail. It probably preyed on fish and squid that swam in the area's shallow seas.

Fibers of connective tissue stretched through the membranes of the pterodactyl's long wings. These batlike membranes were supported by one very long finger in each wing. The fingers were so long, in fact, that they were longer than the animal's body! The animal's bones were thin-walled and hollow, to keep them light for flying.

There's a lot we can't know from fossils, but scientists now think that pterodactyls were probably warm-blooded. Most reptiles, like snakes, lizards, and alligators, are cold-blooded. Warm-blooded reptiles are unusual.

Warm-blooded, hairy, flying reptiles—strange creatures indeed!

BIRDS THAT CAN'T FLY

Ground Bound

What makes a bird a bird? You might say birds are animals that can fly, but that isn't always so. There are more than a dozen species of land birds that can't fly at all.

Long ago, there were some really huge flightless birds. On Madagascar, for example, the elephant bird grew to be nine or ten feet tall. It's thought to have weighed nearly one thousand pounds!

Some large flightless birds of modern times include the ostrich of Africa, the emus and cassowaries of Australia, and the rheas of South America. But none of these birds weighs more than 350 pounds. Not exactly small, but not an elephant bird, either.

You might think that birds this big are flightless because they're so heavy. But some flightless birds are very small. On Stephens Island, off the coast of New Zealand, a tiny wrenlike bird once lived that was only seen to run over the ground like a mouse. It lived in holes in rocks and never flew. Sadly, this bird is now extinct.

Scientists believe all flightless birds are the descendants of birds that could fly. When birds live in a place where there are no predators to hunt them, they don't need their wings to escape. Over time, some species simply lose the ability to fly because they no longer need it.

Many birds that are now extinct were safe until human travelers arrived. These travelers either caught and ate the birds or they brought new predators with them. The last wren seen on Stephens Island was brought in by the light-house keeper's cat.

THE ALBATROSS
Half of Every Year in the Air

The Wandering Albatross spends nearly half of every year, from July to November, flying far out over the oceans of the world, never once touching land.

Most birds fly by using their muscles to flap their wings. But the albatross is the world's largest seabird, spanning ten feet from wing tip to wing tip. If it had to use its muscles to stay aloft, it would need a lot of energy, and staying in the air from November to July would be impossible!

Instead of flapping its wings, the albatross flies using a process called "dynamic soaring." This means that the bird stays in the air by catching the wind in its wings. It takes advantage of changes in wind speed and direction to soar higher or lower, allowing the air to push it up or down.

In addition to dynamic soaring, the albatross uses "slope soaring" to stay in the air. Ocean waves generally move in the direction of the wind, but not as fast. This means that wind flows up the back of each wave, overtaking it. The albatross skims along the ocean surface at high speed, soars up the waves on winds, banks, and then comes back down to catch another upward draft. It doesn't have to flap its wings at all. It can soar for days at a time.

There's almost always wind out at sea. When there's not, the albatross lands on the water and floats until the wind picks up again. The bird won't go back to land until it's time to return to its breeding grounds in the spring.

THE GOLDEN PLOVER
Long-Distance Flyer

Lots of birds spend their summers and winters in different places. Some undertake truly amazing journeys to get from one home to the other. But the golden plover is one of the champion long-distance fliers.

Each spring the summer residents of the tundra—the treeless, frozen plains of the far North—begin to arrive. Among them are the golden plovers. With the long and pointy wings that help them travel great distances, they fly over the tundra in elaborate displays of courtship with their mates, looking for a place to nest and raise their young before heading south again for the next winter. They don't have much time—the summers are short in the far North.

At the end of the summer, golden plovers that have nested all over the tundra gather together in Labrador and Nova Scotia in Canada. Together they take off and fly more than 2,300 miles over the ocean to the coast of Brazil.

After a brief rest in Brazil, the golden plovers fly more than four thousand miles further to the treeless grasslands of Argentina. There they spend their winter.

All that without a map! You might think it would be a good idea, the next spring, to go back to the tundra the same way they came. But the golden plovers don't agree. Instead of retracing their route, they fly north over South and Central America to the Gulf of Mexico, up the Mississippi Valley, then north to their breeding grounds—a trip of nearly eight thousand miles.

All together, golden plovers travel close to fifteen thousand miles in a year. That's quite a lot of flying for a bird that doesn't even weigh half a pound!

THE PENGUIN
Underwater Flyer

Penguins, like other flightless birds, lost the ability to fly long ago because they no longer needed it. But penguins traded in their ability to fly in the air for another talent: flying under water.

On land, penguins are slow moving and awkward—unless they're sledding across the ice and snow on their bellies. But when they slide into the cold ocean waters of the southern hemisphere, where they live, these birds move gracefully.

The wings that once must have carried penguins through the air are now stiff, narrow flippers with scalelike feathers. The long feathers of birds that fly in the air would be of no use at all to penguins, but their scaly flippers are perfect for propelling them rapidly and smoothly through the water as they chase their food.

Because penguins live where it's very cold for most of the year, they have developed special ways to stay warm. Their feather coats are waterproof, and they have a thick layer of body fat for insulation. They also have a built-in heat-exchange system to distribute warmth throughout their bodies, keeping their flippers and legs warm.

Some penguins can dive as deep as eight hundred feet into the icy water and stay under for fifteen minutes or more without breathing. Down there it's very cold, so they really need all of their insulation and waterproofing!

There are other birds that swim well under water, but penguins do something no other bird can. They can swim as porpoises do, gathering speed under water and then bursting up through the surface and into the air, soaring above the waves before going under again. It's quite a sight!

OWLS

Silent Hunters of the Night

Their haunting calls at night tell us they're out there in the darkness, but we almost never see them. And we never hear one flying by. These nighttime hunters are as quiet as a moth!

Owls are extra-quiet fliers because of their especially soft flight feathers. The wing beats of some kinds of owls are so silent they can't even be picked up by finely tuned instruments made to detect sound.

The ability of owls to be silent makes it possible for them to swoop down and capture their prey before being noticed. The prey has no time to escape. Owls that hunt fish, however, are not silent fliers. The fish can't hear them from under the water, so fishing owls don't need to be quiet.

Owls have excellent hearing to help them hunt. They hear so well that they can detect small animals moving around beneath layers of snow. They can't see the animals through the snow, but they can hear that the animals are there. The owls have a special hearing region in the brain that has many nerve cells for sound detection. They also have a wide ear tube and a very large inner ear.

The eyesight of owls is legendary. Their large eyes are designed to gather whatever light is available. This allows them to see very well even in extremely dim light. Because a nighttime sky is never completely dark, owls can hunt with ease throughout the night.

Their stealthful silence, keen vision, and acute hearing have given owls a reputation for wisdom—they always know what's going on. That's why you sometimes hear the expression "wise as an owl."

BATS

Flying Mammals

Mammals don't fly, right? At least not most of them. Some mammals soar—like the "flying" squirrel—jumping and gliding long distances. But one mammal, the bat, actually uses powered flight to stay in the air.

Here's another surprising fact about bats: There are almost one thousand species of bats. They make up nearly one-quarter of all mammal species. This means that in fact, nearly twenty-five percent of all mammal species can fly!

The wings of a bat are made of a membrane that is tightly stretched between the animal's long fingers and forelimbs. On the front of each wing is a clawed thumb used for moving around in the roosts where bats sleep during the day, while most of the rest of the world is awake.

Bats are not blind, but they do use their hearing more than their sight to move around and locate their food. Most bats eat insects, which they track down by a process called "echolocation." This means the bats put out special sounds—similar to radar—that bounce back off their prey. Based on how long it takes for the sound to come back to the bat, it can figure out how far away its prey is.

Other kinds of bats eat other foods, such as fruit, nectar, pollen, fish, frogs, lizards, and even small mammals. And yes, there are vampire bats that eat blood. There are three species of vampire bat that live in South and Central America.

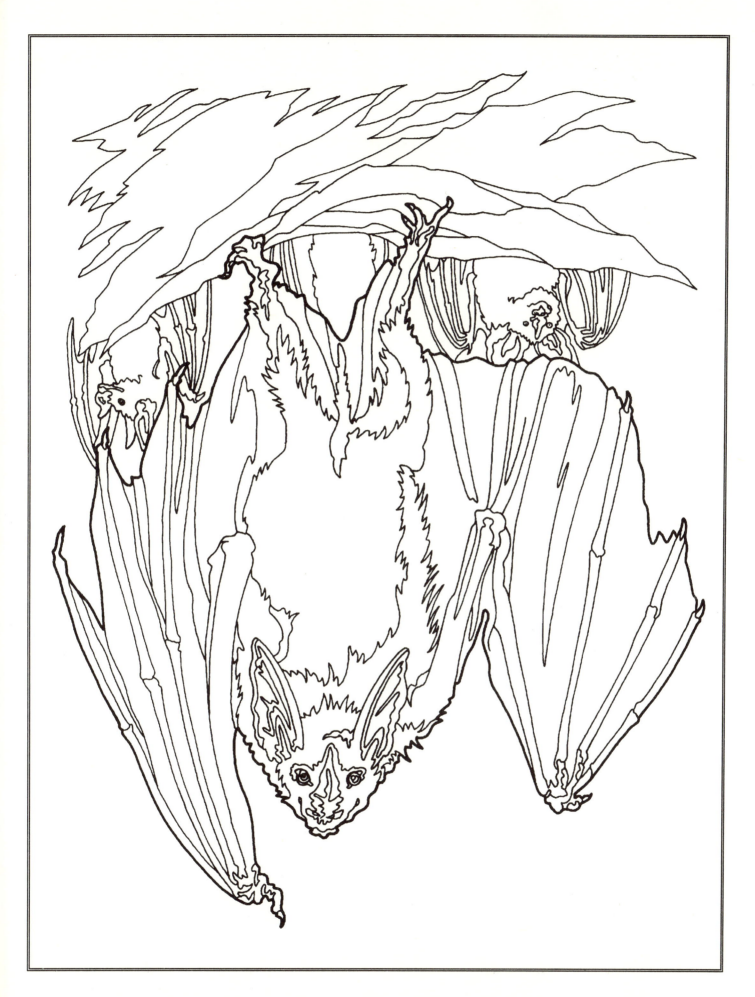

THREE-TOED SLOTHS
The Laziest Animals

Did anyone every tell you that you were being "slothful?" If you wondered what that means, you only have to look at the three-toed sloth to find the answer.

Three-toed sloths live in the rain forests of South and Central America. If you were ever lucky enough to see one, you'd know that they move very, very slowly. They spend most of their lives in trees, just hanging upside down from the branches. Their specialized feet, with claws up to four inches long, are very powerful and can cling fast to a branch for a long time.

During the day, three-toed sloths are motionless. At night they move around a little bit, feeding. Because they only eat leaves, they don't have to move fast or far to find their food—it's right there in the tree with them.

Sloth fur is different from the fur of any other animal in the world. Each long hair has a special groove that runs down the middle. Two different kinds of algae live in these grooves. The algae help hide the sloth from predators by giving it a greenish color that blends in with the trees.

Moths also live in the fur of the three-toed sloth. The sloths move so slowly—when they move at all—that the moths have no trouble keeping up with their mobile homes.

JUMPING MICE

A Long Winter's Nap

When the cold weather of winter arrives, most people just put on more clothes, eat more hot foods to keep warm, and stay inside. Jumping mice, however, live outside and spend their winters in "hibernation."

The seeds and insects that jumping mice and some other hibernators eat are hard to find in the winter. Since they can't find enough food to give them energy for daily activities, they spend the winter in a sort of deep sleep, not eating at all.

If you came across a jumping mouse in its den in the middle of the winter, you might think it was dead. Its breath would be so slow and shallow that it would hardly seem to be breathing at all. Its body temperature would be close to freezing, and its heartbeat would be so slow and faint you might not be able to feel it. During the rest of the year, when the mouse is moving around, its heart beats between five hundred and six hundred times each minute—ten times faster than the human heart. But during hibernation, that rate drops to about thirty beats per minute!

In the fall, to prepare for hibernation, the jumping mouse eats a lot more than usual. In two weeks, it can eat enough to more than double its body weight. This gives it enough food to hibernate, rolled up in a tight little ball, from late September to early May in its cozy, protected den.

SOME ANIMALS THAT HIBERNATE IN THE WILD

Bats

Hedgehogs

Ground Squirrels

Marmots

Hamsters

Fat-tailed Lemurs

Nighthawks

Swifts

Frogs

Toads

Lizards

Snakes

Turtles

SCALLOPS
Shells That See

Scallops are sea creatures that live inside a shell. They are "bivalves," which means they live inside two valves, or shells, that the scallops make out of substances secreted from a skinlike tissue called a "mantle." The mantle of a scallop is different from that of other bivalves because its edges are lined with a row of bright blue eyes. These many eyes don't allow the scallops to see in the way that people do, but they do allow them to detect sudden changes in light. If a hungry starfish creeps up on a scallop for a snack, the scallop will detect the starfish and swim away.

Swimming is another unusual talent of the scallop—not many shells can swim! Scallops have a single strong muscle that can snap their two valves together quickly, forcing water straight out of the shell in a jetlike blast. This blast propels the scallop backward for a distance of two or three feet. If you look inside a scallop shell found at the beach, you can see a scar or indentation where the muscle was attached when the animal was alive.

Scallops can also move in a forward direction by flapping their shells open and shut and directing the jet of water to one side or the other. Some scallops even migrate, swimming off to better feeding grounds when food becomes scarce.

NARWHALS

Unicorns of the Sea

Far to the north, in the oceans of the Arctic Circle, swims a creature even more remarkable than the legendary unicorn. You might have been lucky enough to see a whale swimming in oceans more to the south, but most of us will only see pictures of the narwhal.

Other whales that have teeth, such as the killer whale, have a lot of teeth. The narwhal only has two, and both of them are in its upper jaw. Only one of these teeth grows, but it *really* grows! It comes right out through the whale's upper lip. It then grows outward in a spiral pattern into a straight, grooved tusk that can be nearly ten feet long.

Usually only the male narwhal grows a tusk. Scientists once thought that this tusk was used to break through ice when narwhals got trapped in ice fields. But now we know that when a narwhal needs to break through ice—such as when it needs to come up for air, as all whales must—it breaks through with its forehead. The tusk would probably snap if it were thrust against the ice.

Another idea was that the narwhal used his tusk to probe the ocean floor for food. It's most likely, however, that the tusk is used to fight other males during the mating season, when they compete for mates. Many male narwhals have been found with scars on their heads that appear to have been made by the tusks of other narwhals.

SHARKS
Healthy Appetites

For three hundred million years, these magnificent fish have been swimming the oceans of the world. Some sharks have been huge. The largest ever was *Carcharodon megalodon*, a 25-million-year-old ancestor of today's great white shark. *Carcharodon megalodon* grew up to sixty feet long!

The peaceful whale shark, the largest fish alive in the world today, can be more than fifty feet long. It gets that big eating plankton, squid, and small fish such as sardines and anchovies. This shark is huge, but it's no man-eating monster.

Some sharks do attack people, though. The great white, mako, tiger, and hammerhead sharks all have been known to go after people. These attacks don't happen very often, but when they do they get a lot of publicity.

Sharks will eat just about anything that comes their way. Some of the things that have been found in shark stomachs include: other sharks, fish, lobsters, shells, sea urchins, porpoises, turtles, rays, pigs, dogs, sacks, drums, rope, nails, paper, a bottle of wine, goats, cats, birds, raincoats, car license plates, tin cans, wrist watches, seals, orange peels, a yellow-billed cuckoo, and—of all things—the body of a headless knight still wearing his armor!

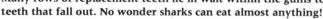

SHARK TEETH

Different kinds of sharks have different kinds of teeth. These include cutting, grasping, crushing, and clutching teeth. The kind of teeth in any shark depends on what kind of prey it eats.

The teeth are set in the gums, rather than in the jaw bones as human teeth are. Many rows of replacement teeth lie in wait within the gums to take the place of teeth that fall out. No wonder sharks can eat almost anything!

Sand shark

Cow shark

Lemon shark

Tiger shark

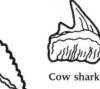

Cow shark

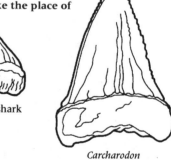

Carcharodon megalodon

Top to bottom: Hammerhead shark, Bull shark, Tiger shark, Blue shark.

THE DUCK-BILLED PLATYPUS

Amazing Animal of Australia

A poisonous, egg-laying mammal with a bill like a duck's—who ever heard of such a creature? The duck-billed platypus is certainly one of nature's more amazing wonders.

This strange creature can be found in Australia. It swims in streams, rivers, and lakes, and makes burrows in their banks. As it dives underwater, the short and very dense fur of the duck-billed platypus keeps it warm. It closes its eyes and ears and makes use of its soft and sensitive ducklike bill to get around.

The bill of the platypus is covered with a black, shiny skin that has a lot of nerve endings. It helps the platypus detect and avoid obstacles such as fallen logs when the animal swims with its eyes closed. The bill also helps locate food, such as insect larvae—a favorite treat—or crayfish, shrimp, snails, tadpoles, worms, and small fish.

The male platypus is one of the few mammals that can produce a venom—a poisonous fluid. A horny, hollow spur on the back of the platypus's ankle can deliver enough venom to kill a dog or seriously injure a person.

The duck-billed platypus was once in danger of becoming very rare or even extinct. It was hunted for its beautiful fur. But now the Australian government protects the animals through a conservation program, and there are once again many duck-billed platypuses to be found in Australia.

WATER STRIDERS
Bugs with Floating Footsteps

If you've ever sat by a pond, lake, or stream on a still summer's day, you may have noticed groups of a particular kind of bug moving across the surface of the water as if they were ice skating. In fact these bugs, known as "water striders," are walking on water.

The water strider can dart rapidly across the water on its long and stiltlike back legs without ever sinking in or getting wet. Its feet make little indentations in the water, but they never break through the surface film.

Water striders take advantage of one of the most interesting properties of water. Water molecules are strongly attracted to each other—they stick very tightly together. This allows water to support objects that are heavier than it is. The attraction between water molecules is part of the reason people can float on water. It's also the reason water striders can skate across the surface without sinking.

Water striders are always looking for something to eat. They feed mostly on small insects that have fallen out of the air and become stuck in the surface film of the water. As these insects struggle to get back into the air, they send out ripples over the surface of the water. The water striders detect the motion of the ripples and follow them to their next meal.

There are some other bugs that can walk on water, such as "water boatmen" and "back swimmers," but these bugs spend a lot of their time swimming, too. The water strider never gets wet.

SPIDERS

Spinners of Silk That's Harder Than Steel

Did you know that a single thread of spider silk is stronger than a thread of steel of the same thickness?

Spider silk is very strong. It also holds up in all kinds of weather. For instance, spider silk doesn't dissolve in water. That's why, if you go outside in the early morning, you can find dozens of glistening spider webs clinging to the grass, wet with dew that reflects the morning light.

Spiders have silk glands in their abdomens. Inside these glands they make a liquid form of silk. When a spider pushes the liquid silk out into the air—through openings called "spinnerets"—the silk hardens into a fine thread. This is how spiders get the silk to spin their webs.

All spiders have different kinds of glands for making different kinds of silk. Some silk becomes completely dry in the air, while some stays sticky to catch insects for the spider to eat. Spiders can mix different kinds of silk together for different kinds of structures and purposes. Some spiders can even make beaded threads of silk—very good for catching jumping or flying insects—by letting go of the thread with a snap.

All spiders make silk, but not all spiders spin webs. One spider, called a "bolus spider," throws a single line of sticky silk—like a lasso—out to capture its prey. You might call the bolus a spider cowboy!

A Wolf spider and a garden spider.

SPIDER WEBS
Wispy Woven Wonders

A spider can make its web in about an hour. To begin, it spins a thread and sends it out into the breeze until the thread catches on an object such as a twig or a flower. This first line serves as a bridge and starts the foundation for the rest of the web. The spider pulls it tight and fastens it firmly. Then the spider sends out other foundation lines into the breeze to build the frame of the web. The foundation lines form the outside edge of the web.

When the foundation lines are in place, the spider begins making "radius lines." These run from one foundation line to another, through the center of the web, like the spokes of a wheel. The spider starts at one foundation line and moves to the line across from it, releasing a thread as it goes. When it gets to the other foundation line, it attaches the radius line and pulls it tight. It then goes back along the radius line, releasing a new thread that sticks to the old one, making it stronger. Then the spider moves to the other side of the web, on another foundation line, and begins another radius thread.

Eventually the spider weaves many radius threads that meet at a hub in the center. Then it spins a spiral thread across all the radial threads, to hold them in place. Finally it spins a very sticky thread in a spiral from the outside of the web all the way to the hub, leaving a clear zone at the very center. And then it settles down in the center, head pointing down, waiting patiently for its next meal to wander into the web and get caught on the sticky threads.

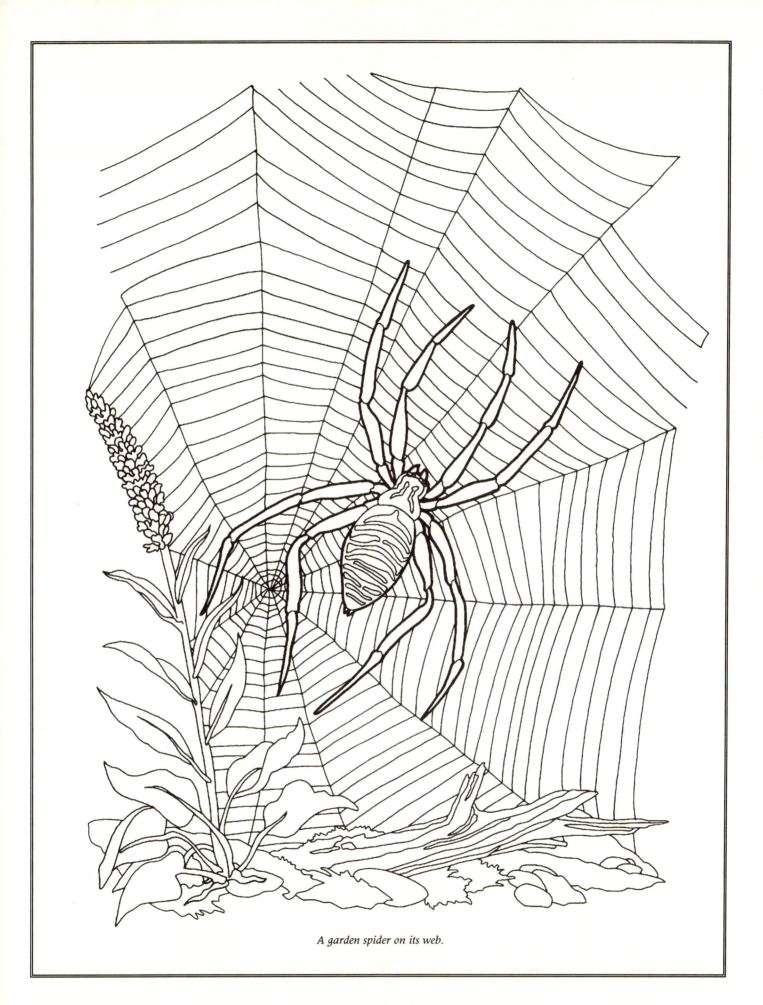

A garden spider on its web.

FIREFLIES
Living Night Lights

You can see them outside at night on a warm summer evening—little lights floating and bobbing in the darkness.

Fireflies, or lightning bugs, are not actually flies. They're beetles. And they're certainly not made of fire or lightning!

There are 1,900 different species of lightning bugs, found on every continent except Antarctica. The larvae, or young, of all species of firefly light up. For this reason, the larvae are called "glowworms." Most adult fireflies also light up. In some species, even the eggs glow!

Adult fireflies flash their green, orange, or yellow lights on and off in an effort to attract mates. Each species of firefly has its own signal for this purpose.

The lights of these beetles give off almost no heat. In fact, if you had a tiny candle flame the size of a firefly's light, the candle flame would be 80,000 times hotter!

In the Waitomo Caves of New Zealand, one species of firefly gives visitors a spectacular show. On the ceiling of these caves, high above an underground river, live many thousands of brightly shining glowworms. Hanging from each glowworm is a long silken thread, looking like a festive streamer decorating the ceiling. Insects that fly into these threads get stuck and become dinner for the larvae.

The beautiful lights of the Waitomo glowworms make the caves dazzle and give them a magical, enchanted look, bringing tourists from all over the world.

SINGING CATERPILLARS
What Are They Singing, Anyhow?

There are a lot of strange and wonderful things on Earth, but who would have thought of a singing caterpillar?

A beautiful butterfly known as *Thisbe irenea* lives in Panama. A biologist studying this butterfly discovered that its caterpillars, the larvae that eventually grow up to be butterflies, actually do sing—ever so softly.

These caterpillars live in association with ants. The ants actively and aggressively protect the caterpillars from predators that hunt them. *Thisbe* caterpillars are a favorite food for wasps. Female wasps like to feed these caterpillars to their young.

Ants are the enemies of the wasp, so the caterpillars are much safer with them around. To keep the ants nearby, *Thisbe* caterpillars sing. They move their heads in and out, sliding them against what are known as "papillae." These are delicate rods with a series of grooves around them. The caterpillars' heads are covered with small bumps that look like guitar picks. These bumps slide across the grooves of the papillae and produce a faint sound. The sound causes a vibration that attracts the ants.

As an extra reward for its ant protectors, each *Thisbe* caterpillar has special organs that secrete a nectar that ants love to eat. The ants lick this nutritious food right off the caterpillar's body. The caterpillars are kept safe, the ants are well fed, and everyone is happy—except maybe the wasps!

MONARCH BUTTERFLIES

Marvelous Migrators

Monarch butterflies are a favorite part of anybody's summer. We see them flying over fields and hovering around milkweed flowers. They lay their eggs on this plant so their larvae can dine on the leaves.

In early fall, you may have seen groups or whole flocks of monarchs flying by. Monarchs are cold-blooded and can't fly if their temperature falls below 86 degrees Fahrenheit, so they migrate to warmer places when it gets cold.

Some monarchs fly all the way from Canada to Mexico—more than two thousand miles, which seems like a pretty long trip for a butterfly. Lots of birds make trips that long, but monarchs only weigh one-fiftieth of an ounce! They don't have enough fat to store the energy they would need to flap their wings the whole way to Mexico. Instead, they glide.

Monarchs are excellent gliders. They have very small bodies and much larger wings. They rise into the sky on heated air currents and drift for long distances, never flapping their wings. For each half mile a monarch rises into the air, it can drift about two miles before it has floated down to its original altitude. Then it has to fly up again. In addition, these skillful gliders are very good at riding the tail winds, which push them south much faster.

When they arrive at their winter homes, the monarchs gather together in trees by the thousands. Sometimes trees in Central America can be seen completely coated with the glorious orange and black migrators!

LEAF-CUTTING ANTS

Fungus Farmers

Do you like mushrooms? Mushrooms are a kind of fungus. Some ants in Central and South America like one kind of fungus so much that they farm it and never eat anything else.

Leaving their underground colonies, where as many as several million ants live together, the tiny farmers travel in a single-file line to a tree or large bush. They climb up the tree or bush and cut off small pieces of leaves. Sometimes they cut off every leaf in the tree.

On their way back home, each ant carries a little piece of leaf on its head. If you saw them you might think they were leaf *eaters*. But they're called "leaf-cutting ants" for a reason.

When they get back to their underground nest, the ants each take a piece of leaf into a special chamber. There they cut the leaf piece into still smaller pieces which they chew up thoroughly, mixing them with saliva and then pushing them into the bottom of the chamber. There they add some bits of fungus to the chewed up leaves.

After a few days, the fungus grows little round tips—just like mushrooms. The ants pick these tips and eat them for breakfast, lunch, and dinner. Every day.

Scientists think the fungus eaten by the leaf-cutting ants has been farmed by them for millions of years. It is almost never found growing by itself, and it's extremely difficult to make it grow in a laboratory without the leaf-cutters' help. It seems like the ant depends on the fungus and the fungus depends on the ant. Neither one can live without the other.

MEAT-EATING PLANTS

Hungry Vegetables

If you've ever had a vegetable garden, you know all too well that many insects like to eat plants. Flowers, fruits, and leaves of all sorts can be attacked by plant-eating insects. But sometimes it's the other way around. . . .

Carnivorous, or meat-eating, plants are found all over the world, but only in special places. They usually live in bogs or swamps, or other places where the soil has very little nitrogen in it.

Nitrogen is a chemical that plants need to grow, and insects have nitrogen in their bodies. So if a plant lives in an area where the soil has very little nitrogen, one thing it can do is devise clever ways of catching insects.

Some meat-eating plants have tube-shaped leaves. These are known as "pitcher plants." Rainwater sits at the bottom of these leaves, and any insect that comes down the tube drowns. Then the plant secretes a digestive fluid that dissolves the insect so the plant can eat it.

"Sundews," another kind of meat-eating plant, have leaves with sticky hairs on them. When an insect gets stuck on the hairs, the sides of the leaf curl up to hold it in place while the plant eats it.

Probably the most famous carnivorous plant is the "Venus' flytrap." This plant looks like it has a "mouth" that's made of two folded leaves with a series of teethlike spikes that point inward. The surface of the leaves is covered with trigger hairs. When an insect touches one of these hairs, the "mouth" snaps shut, trapping the insect behind the spikes until it gets digested by the plant.

The good news is that carnivorous plants only eat bugs—never people!

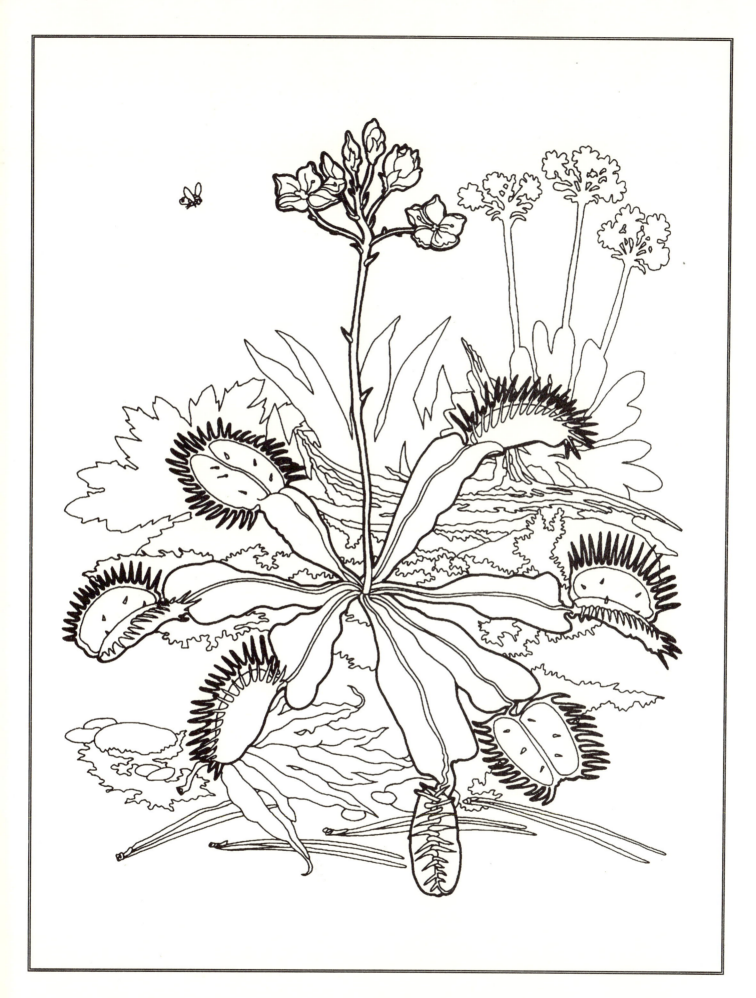

MIRROR, MIRROR, ON THE WALL

As you read through this book and colored in pictures of the world's natural wonders, you probably found lots of interesting things to think about. You may have remembered a visit to Niagara Falls or a time when you explored a cave. Perhaps you wondered what it would be like to visit Antarctica and throw boiling water up into the air. You might have dreamed about seeing a narwhal.

That's a pretty amazing gift—the ability to think, remember, wonder, and dream. Human beings are natural wonders, too, just as surely as singing caterpillars or glowing worms. People can write great poems or scary mysteries. We can sing and laugh at silly jokes until we cry. We can paint pictures and make all sorts of useful things: cars, matches, bread, blankets, and spaceships.

You can probably think of dozens of other unique and wonderful things that only humans can do. If you and a friend each wrote down a separate list of such things, your lists would not be the same. We're all the same in many ways, but each of us is also very different from everyone else. Every human being in the world has unique characteristics and special talents. There's no one else just like you anywhere. Isn't that wonderful?

Inside this frame you can draw a picture of yourself, your favorite natural wonder,
or something you think is more amazing than anything in this book!

THE AGE OF DINOSAURS
by Donald F. Glut

Discover new theories about dinosaurs and learn how paleontologists work in this fascinating expedition to a time when reptiles ruled the land.

THE AMERICAN WEST
by Emmanuel M. Kramer

Explore the lives and legends of the American West—with 60 images to color.

ARCHITECTURE
by Peter Dobrin

Tour 60 world-famous buildings around the globe and learn their stories.

AUDUBON'S BIRDS OF AMERICA
by George S. Glenn, Jr.

Read about the adventures of naturalist and artist John James Audubon, and let your imagination soar with this field trip to the fantastic world of American birds.

BULFINCH'S MYTHOLOGY
Retold by Steven Zorn

An excellent introduction to classical literature, with 16 tales of adventure.

FOLKTALES OF NATIVE AMERICANS
Retold by David Borgenicht

Traditional myths, tales, and legends, from more than 12 Native American peoples.

FORESTS
by Elizabeth Corning Dudley, Ph.D.

Winner, Parents' Choice "Learning and Doing Award"

The first ecological coloring book, written by a respected botanist.

GRAY'S ANATOMY
by Fred Stark, Ph.D.

Winner, Parents' Choice "Learning and Doing Award"

A voyage of discovery through the human body, based on the classic work.

INSECTS
by George S. Glenn, Jr.

Discover the secrets of familiar and more unusual insects.

MASTERPIECES
by Mary Martin and Steven Zorn

Line drawings and lively descriptions of 60 world-famous paintings and their artists.

OCEANS
by Diane M. Tyler and James C. Tyler, Ph.D.

Winner, Parents' Choice "Learning and Doing Award"

An exploration of the life-giving seas, in expert text and 60 pictures.

PLACES OF MYSTERY
by Emmanuel M. Kramer

An adventurous tour of the most mysterious places on Earth, with more than 50 stops along the way.